# ECLAIR

MW00944555

A Sandy Bay Cozy Mystery

*By*

*Amber Crewes*

*Amber Crewes*

For questions and comments about this book, please contact info@ambercrewes.com

**www.AmberCrewes.com**

ISBN:  9781072504399
Imprint: Independently Published

# Eclairs and Lethal Layers

# Other books in the Sandy Bay Series

Eclairs and Lethal Layers

A

# Sandy Bay

## COZY MYSTERY

# Book Five

Amber Crewes

# 1

IF SUCCESS HAD A TASTE, Meghan Truman was sure it'd taste like one of her desserts. Despite the many challenges her business had faced since its inception, she could confidently say it was a success, both in terms of the health of its finances and its reputation in the area. She was hopeful that her business would go from strength to strength and she welcomed the challenge to exceed her customers' expectations.

It was a gray, windy morning, but she did not mind; while as a recent transplant from sunny Los Angeles, Meghan had not anticipated enjoying the weather of the Pacific Northwest, she found that the cool mornings and dark skies made her feel cozy and relaxed. She loved snuggling into thick, chunky sweaters and her knee-high boots, and in spite of the occasional rainstorm, Meghan felt more at home in Sandy Bay than she had ever felt in Los Angeles.

"It's a great day to be in Sandy Bay!" Meghan

chirped to Fiesta and Siesta, her little twin dogs as they playfully nipped at her heels as she prepared for the day. "The sun isn't shining, and from my window, the sea looks rough, but I can just tell that it's going to be a good day, my sweet puppers!"

Meghan smiled at her reflection in the mirror. Her dark, wavy hair was pulled back into a messy bun at the nape of her neck, and her deep brown eyes sparkled as she applied a layer of ballet pink lip gloss to her thick, bow-shaped lips. Meghan reached into her drawer to retrieve an apron, and she smoothed down the wrinkled front as she walked down the narrow staircase, both dogs following her as she entered the kitchen of Truly Sweet, her bakery.

The wind rattled the small, silvers bells attached to the front door of Truly Sweet, and she glanced up and smiled as a statuesque, curly-haired woman walked through the door. It was a quiet Tuesday morning, and the bakery had only been open for ten minutes, rendering Meghan pleasantly surprised to see someone stepping across the threshold of her shop.

"Good morning!" she chimed to the stranger as the woman approached the counter. Meghan could see that they were around the same age, and her smile widened; Karen, her dearest friend in her adopted hometown of Sandy Bay, was over seventy years old, and Meghan was eager to make some friends closer to her age; her former assistant, Lori, was close to her age, but had recently left for college, and Meghan brimmed with excitement as she studied the attractive young woman staring at her from across the counter.

"Hi," replied the woman, tucking a loose brunette lock behind her ear. "I'm Stephanie Cameron, and I'm new here to Sandy Bay. I've done some asking around; it's a small town, as you know, and everyone seems willing to give me every detail of every person in town. I hear that you're new to Sandy Bay as well?"

Meghan nodded enthusiastically. "I am." she responded giddily. "My name is Meghan Truman and I moved here a few months ago, so I know the lay of the land pretty well, but I'm not a native Sandy Bay-er. What brings you to town, Stephanie?"

Stephanie bit her lip and looked down at the wooden floor. "I'm from Indiana," she began. "My husband and I split up; I was an investment banker in Indianapolis and living the dream. But, some dreams come to an end…."

Meghan's lips turned down. "I'm so sorry to hear that," she said softly. "I'm sure Sandy Bay is very different than Indiana; I've never been, but I hear it's very flat there."

Stephanie nodded. "Very flat, and we have a lot of corn."

Meghan smiled. "We don't have a lot of corn here, but we have some gorgeous beaches, and the weather is just to die for! You can curl up with tea and a good book any day of the week, and it's always sweater weather in Sandy Bay."

Stephanie bit her lip. "That does sound nice," she

said. "I'm hoping for a real change, and I think the Pacific Northwest is where I'll find it. I hope…."

Meghan nodded. "I hope Sandy Bay is the perfect place for you to have a fresh beginning. I came here from Los Angeles and didn't have a lot going for *me,* but *now*…." Meghan opened her arms to gesture at the counters and displays in the bakery. "Now, I have Truly Sweet, *and* some wonderful friends here."

Stephanie smiled at Meghan, showing one thick dimple etched into the side of her face. "That's actually what I came here to chat with you about…."

Meghan cocked her head to the side. "Oh?"

Stephanie nodded. "I got into town a few weeks ago, and I've actually been thinking about starting my *own* bakery. I've done some research, and from what I've read, Sandy Bay is an ideal place to open a bakery."

Meghan grinned. "That's wonderful," she cried. "It's a truly sweet business to be in. I was *lost* until I started my business here, and I'm so excited that you'll have the same luck I did. Do you have any experience running a bakery?"
Stephanie shook her head. "No," she said quietly. "That's actually why I came to see you. I was at the grocery store last night, and when I chatted with the bag-boy, he mentioned that you were a nice girl with a new bakery. I just *had* to stop by and meet you. Can I ask you a huge favor?"

Meghan nodded. "I remember what it was like to be new in town," she answered, placing a hand on her heart and remembering the rocky beginning to her new life in Sandy Bay. "I'm happy to help. What can I do for you?"

Stephanie gestured at one of the little white iron tables in the corner. "Can we sit? Honestly, I want to pick your brain. I've always *dreamed* of starting my own bakery, but I don't know how to begin. I don't want to step on your toes; you seem like a nice girl, and I realize a new bakery would be competition, but do you think we could just chat a little about *your* experiences here in Sandy Bay?"

Meghan nodded. She had seen the hurt in Stephanie's eyes when Stephanie had mentioned her failed marriage, and Meghan knew how important it was to welcome newcomers to town.

"Absolutely!" Meghan exclaimed as Stephanie's eyes lit up. "Let me grab some treats for us; it's early, and I think some tea and fresh croissants would just be the coziest."

Ten minutes later, Meghan and Stephanie were laughing over the warm, soft croissants that Meghan had baked earlier that morning. Meghan leaned back in her chair, delighted to be advising Stephanie, who was proving to be good company.

"A bakery is like one of these croissants," Meghan giggled, licking her lips. "A bakery has many layers; there is the business layer of things, the merchandise, and the customers you have the pleasure to serve."

Stephanie smiled warmly. "That's a great way to

think about it," she said, reaching over and patting Meghan on the hand. "It's been so kind of you to sit down with me about this; I was *so* nervous to come ask, but you've been such a dear."

Meghan beamed, her dark eyes shining. "I'm just happy that you're here. Sandy Bay is lovely, Stephanie; it's on the coast, the town is quiet, for the most part, and people here will embrace what you have to offer. I just know it!"

Stephanie nodded. "It's like you said, a bakery is about layers. That makes so much sense to me."

Meghan agreed. "If your customers know you, like you, and *trust* you, you'll get it right," she assured Stephanie. "With those layers, success is guaranteed!"

Stephanie glanced down at her watch, her eyes widening. "Oh, goodness! I have a meeting with my new finance guy in ten minutes. I'm sorry to cut this short, Meghan, but I'm so glad we got to chat."

Meghan rose to her feet and leaned in to hug Stephanie. "Don't be a stranger. Like I said, I'm always happy to help those who are new in town. Swing by any time you'd like."

Stephanie waved as she walked out of the bakery and into the sunny morning. "I will! Thanks, Meghan!"

Meghan sighed happily as the little silver bells attached to the front door of the bakery chimed as Stephanie left. "There was my good deed for the day, and it isn't even ten in the morning yet" she laughed to herself, running a hand through her long, dark hair and adjusting the white apron around her waist. "She seemed like a great girl. I hope I didn't tell her too much, though; maybe she had a point about being competition to *my* bakery...."

# 2

TWO WEEKS LATER, Meghan's mouth was agape as she stood in the dining area of Truly Sweet, her bakery. From the front window, she could see a long line of people outside of *Duly Doux*, Stephanie Cameron's bakery. Stephanie had chosen a vacant building just across the street to open her own shop, and now, Meghan felt her body grow cold as she peered across the street at the smiling faces gathered outside of Duly Doux. Truly Sweet hadn't seen a customer all morning, and Meghan's heart pounded as she calculated how much business she had lost since Stephanie's doors had opened three hours before.

"It *must* be the novelty of a new establishment in town. It *must* be!" Meghan reassured herself as she saw Karen Denton, her close friend, step into the line outside of Duly Doux. "It's nice the people in Sandy Bay are supporting Stephanie. I'm *happy* for her."

A few moments later, as Meghan tried to bury herself in baking, she heard the tinny chime of the bells ring

as someone walked into the bakery. "Hello?" Meghan

called out from the kitchen, thrilled to have someone to serve. "Good morning! Welcome to Truly Sweet." Meghan dashed into the dining area to find Sally Sheridan glaring at her. Mrs. Sheridan was known in town for being fussy and mean, and Meghan forced herself to smile politely as Mrs. Sheridan impatiently tapped her cane on the wooden floor.

"Well, hello there, Mrs. Sheridan." she said sweetly. "What a pleasant surprise to see you. Can I help you with something today?"

Mrs. Sheridan shook her head and narrowed her eyes at Meghan. "I want to make a return," she announced, her head held high as she slung a small, unfamiliar paper sack on the counter.

"I beg your pardon," Meghan began carefully. "But that bag is not from my bakery. What is in there, Mrs. Sheridan?"

Mrs. Sheridan used her cane to point at Duly Doux. "It's from *that* bakery," she explained in her raspy voice. "Duly Doux. Doux means sweet in French, did you know that, Meghan?"

Meghan bit her lip, but pasted the smile back on her face. "I do now," she said. "Mrs. Sheridan? Why are you bringing items from another bakery in to make a return *here*? I can't do that for you."

Mrs. Sheridan's lips turned upward into a rare smile. "Just try what's in there," Mrs. Sheridan prompted. Meghan obediently reached into the sack and pulled out an éclair.

"It looks delicious," she admitted, slowly biting into the pastry. "It tastes *just* like my éclairs though, Mrs. Sheridan! I even taste some cinnamon in this pastry; that's my secret ingredient for éclairs!"

Mrs. Sheridan smirked at Meghan and rapped her cane on the floor. "It's better than one of yours," she declared. "Everyone across the street is saying so! That line is winding around the block, and I just thought you should know about this, Meghan. And, I'd like to make my return."

Meghan shook her head. "No," she said firmly. "I will not allow you to *return* an item that didn't even come from *my* bakery. I'm sorry, Mrs. Sheridan, but that just won't do."

Mrs. Sheridan rolled her eyes at Meghan and turned away from the counter. "You're too stiff for your own good, Meghan," she said. "That Stephanie girl was a real nice lady. You better be careful, girl; if you aren't nice to your customers, Truly Sweet might just lose out to Duly Doux…."

Meghan held back harsh words as Mrs. Sheridan hobbled out of the bakery.
"That was so rude," she muttered under her breath. "I'm *happy* for Stephanie. I'm *happy* to have shared some of my experiences with someone new. I just need to stay positive, and everything will be okay."

Meghan returned to her work and began cutting up thick, red slices of rhubarb for a fresh pie. "I just have to stay *positive*," she repeated to herself as she admired the long, perfect stalks of rhubarb. "I just have to keep my chin up."

As Meghan sliced through the rhubarb, she heard her cell phone begin to ring. "It's Karen," she said to herself as she answered the call. "Hi, Karen! How was Duly Doux?"

"It was good," she admitted. "It was *fabulous,* even! You know that I don't eat sweets often; with my marathon coming up next week, I really shouldn't have indulged, but Stephanie's desserts were very good."

Meghan laughed. "You're the only person over fifty I know who runs marathons, Karen. How do you do it?"

Karen giggled. "It keeps me young, sweetie. Anyway, I had a quick question for you; did you share your éclair recipe with Stephanie? I had a taste of one of hers, and it tasted just like *yours*!"
The hairs stood up on Meghan's arms as she frowned. "No," she said. "I didn't share *any* recipes with her. She didn't ask for recipes; she only asked me for some business advice."

Karen paused. "That's strange," she finally replied. "When I took a bite of the éclair, I asked her if she had talked with you about your secret recipe, and she said that you had shared some of your favorite recipes with *her*...."

Meghan's heart began to pound. "I didn't share with her, but my cookbook was on the counter when she stopped by," she said slowly as she remembered the morning of Stephanie's visit. "I turned my back to fetch tea and croissants for us….maybe she copied down some of my recipes when I wasn't looking!"

Karen groaned. "I hate to hear that, sweetie," she said. "Stephanie seems so nice. We had a fabulous chat while I was in there, and I'm disappointed to hear *this*."

Meghan sighed. "It sounds like I may need to pay her a visit. My recipes are for *my* customers! I'm happy to share tips and advice, but I can't have Stephanie jeopardizing my livelihood by stealing my recipes."

"I agree," Karen said. "Just be careful; she is new in town, and maybe there's been a misunderstanding, sweetie. Just be kind and be *truly sweet*; this could all be resolved by a little chat. Just hang in there."

"I will," she promised. "I will."

After Meghan and Karen hung up the phone, the bakery's main line began to ring. "Hello?" Meghan answered.

"Ms. Truman? This is Dave Dane at Majestic Incorporated? I wanted to touch base regarding the corporate order we placed last week. Is now a good time?"

Meghan smiled. Receiving the Majestic Incorporated corporate order had been a huge milestone for the bakery; the company was an internationally acclaimed tape conglomerate, and Meghan knew the order would significantly advance her business.

"No problem, Mr. Dane," Meghan cooed. "So happy to hear from you. I received the order last week and have been busy preparing the first shipment of treats to send over."

Meghan heard Mr. Dane sigh. "I'm sorry to tell you this, Ms. Truman, but we are going to have to retract our order."
"What?" she cried. "You are cancelling the order?"

"I apologize for any inconvenience, but due to recent developments, we have decided to go a different direction with our order. You will of course be compensated for your initial efforts, but we will no longer be requiring your services."

"I'm sorry to hear that," she replied flatly. "Please let me know if that changes. Thank you."

As Meghan hung up the phone, her hands began to shake, and she felt thick, hot tears welling up in her dark eyes. "I barely have any business today, Mrs. Sheridan taunted me, Stephanie may have *stolen* my recipe for my special éclairs, and Majestic Incorporated cancelled my corporate order! What *else* could possibly go wrong today?"

# 3

MEGHAN NERVOUSLY GRIPPED the straps of her red leather purse as she and Karen walked across the street to Duly Doux. It was a chilly afternoon; the harsh, salty winds from the Pacific were blowing mercilessly into town, and Meghan shivered as the cool air cut through her thin coat.

"Don't be nervous," Karen ordered as they arrived outside of Duly Doux. "From what we know, Stephanie *stole* your éclair recipe! I know you don't like confrontation, but this is unacceptable behavior, especially from someone who sought help from you only days ago!"

Meghan nodded. "I know," she breathed softly. "I know, Karen. I need to do a better job at standing up for myself. I just don't want to jump to conclusions. Stephanie moved to Sandy Bay for a fresh start, and who knows if this all isn't just a big coincidence?"

Karen stared into Meghan's dark eyes. "Meghan," she began. "Stephanie *told* me that *you* gave her your secret recipe! I didn't mishear her. We need to get to the bottom of this; I *hate* thieves and cheats, and you don't deserve to have your kindness wasted. Come on!"

Karen turned on her heel and strode into Duly Doux. The shop was bustling with customers, and Stephanie smiled warmly from behind the counter as Meghan and Karen approached her.

"Meghan! Karen! What a surprise!" Stephanie cooed, tossing her hair behind her shoulder as Meghan glanced around at the crowded bakery. "What can I do for you two ladies today?"

Karen glared at the owner of Duly Doux. "Stephanie," she hissed. "When I was in here the other day, you mentioned that dear Meghan had *given* you the recipe to her wonderful eclairs…."

Stephanie's eyes widened as she looked over at Meghan's face. "Ummm….I didn't quite say that, Karen. You must have heard me wrong."

Karen leaned across the counter. She was only inches from Stephanie's nose, and she took a long, deep inhale. "Are you sure?"

Looking horrified, Stephanie leaned away from Karen and shook her head. "Meghan? Can you get your friend under control? I don't know what she's talking about. I seem to recall saying that I *wish* you would share some of your recipes with me, but I never said you *did* share them."

Meghan raised an eyebrow. "Oh? I've heard that some of our desserts taste very, *very* similar, Stephanie. Can you help me understand why that is?"

Stephanie folded her arms across her chest and looked nervously at Meghan. "I don't think this is a good time," she whispered, jerking her chin to gesture at the customers who had grown quiet and were now watching the three women interact. "Can we take this outside?"

"Stephanie!"

All three women turned to see a short, plump woman emerge from the back room. "Stephanie, where are those recipes you copied down? I'm about to make another batch of the eclairs, and I need the recipes you copied down so I can make them the way you told me to."

Stephanie turned and frowned at the woman. "Not now, Trudy…."

Trudy shrugged. "I'm just trying to be a helpful assistant, Stephanie! Come on! I followed the directions perfectly earlier. You told me to make the eclairs exactly as you had written down the recipe, and I did."

Stephanie's face paled. "This is not a good time, Trudy! Please go wait for me in the back."

Trudy rolled her eyes, but she obediently left the counter and returned to the backroom where she had come from.

"What was that all about?" Karen demanded. "What was she referring to, Stephanie? Just tell the truth! We know that you copied down Meghan's recipes without her permission, and we want to hear the truth!"

Stephanie pursed her lips. "What I am making for *my* customers is none of your business," she said coolly. "I'm sorry that your little bakery hasn't seen much success since Duly Doux opened, but I can't help the fact that my treats are made better."

"You treats are made *just as mine are*!" Meghan shouted as Karen's face shone with pride. "I know you copied down my recipes! Just admit it, Stephanie!"

Stephanie smirked. "Or what? What are you going to do, Meghan?"

Karen balled her hands into fists. Meghan's eyes widened as Karen's impressive biceps bulged out from beneath her tight athletic top. "What is she going to do?" Karen taunted. "More like what she won't do. You picked the wrong girl to mess with, Stephanie; Meghan has worked hard to perfect her recipes and earn her client base, and I won't stand by while you steal from her! I hate thieves, and this makes me *sick*!"

Stephanie narrowed her eyes. "Get out of my bakery!"

Karen batted her eyelashes. "Gladly," she said. "I do yoga, Stephanie; I don't believe in violence, but I wish I could just snuff the life out of you and this terrible shop. People like you make me sick. How dare you take advantage of my fabulous friend, Meghan?"

"Get out before I call the police," Stephanie ordered. "Now!"

Meghan and Karen shot Stephanie one last frustrated look and then left the shop. "I'm proud of you," Karen said to Meghan as she pulled her into a hug. "You stood up for yourself, and from what we could see, it's pretty clear that Stephanie had something to hide. You don't act that nasty if you are innocent, I know that for sure."

Meghan shook her head. "I just don't understand how she could be so rude."

Karen bit her lip. "I could just kill her," she said. "Your recipes and your bakery are the *best* Sandy Bay has ever seen! I hope her silly shop folds up soon. She *deserves* it."

Meghan smiled at Karen. "Thanks for going with me. You help make me brave, Karen."

Karen shook her head. "You're brave on your own, Meghan," she replied. "You're brave on your own."

\*\*\*\*\*\*\*\*\*\*

The next morning, Meghan awoke to the sounds of sirens outside of her window. She rubbed her eyes and tiptoed out of bed, careful not to disturb Fiesta and Siesta, her two tiny twin dogs who had been curled up on both sides of Meghan's body.

"What is that sound?" Meghan groaned as she peered through the blinds and looked out upon the street. Firetrucks and ambulances were parked carelessly along the sidewalk, and Meghan gasped as she saw the coroner's truck pull in.

"What's going on?" she said aloud as she watched Trudy, Stephanie's assistant, walk outside of Duly Doux, her face red and her body shaking. The coroner walked up to her and placed a hand on her shoulder. Trudy turned and led the coroner inside of the bakery.

"Oh no…." Meghan muttered. She threw on a bathrobe and slippers and ran downstairs. She spotted Jack Irvin, the handsome, tall, blonde police detective she had been dating for the last few months, and she ran into his arms.

"Meghan!" Jack said in surprise. "What are you doing out here?"

Meghan looked into Jack's blue eyes. "What's going on?"

Jack sighed. "There's been a death, Meghan. I can't say much more."

Meghan nodded. "I understand," she said, surveying the police and EMTs running in and out of Duly Doux. "Is there anything you can tell me?"

Suddenly, Trudy burst out of the bakery, tears streaming down her face. "She's dead!" Trudy bawled. "Stephanie is dead! Someone *strangled* Stephanie!"

# 4

EVERY DAY COMES WITH its unique package of surprises and opportunities. Some are welcome, while some are not. Meghan's package, so far today, had been very unwelcome.

"Okay, Meghan, I think you're good to go," Jack said as Meghan buried her face in her hands.

The couple sat across from each other in a windowless room at the Sandy Bay Police Station, and Meghan was exhausted from nearly two hours of Jack's rapid-fire questioning.

"He is a thorough detective," Meghan had thought to herself as Jack read his questions from the notepad. "I hate that I'm here, but I'm so impressed with what Jack can do…."

A few hours after Meghan had awoken to the sirens outside of her apartment, Jack had collected her for questioning. "It's standard," he assured her as he ushered her into his police car. "You live right across the street from the murder scene, and with your close proximity, Officer Nunan thought it best that we talk."

Meghan had nodded and complied with Jack's request. She had not been concerned about talking at the police station; she had been sound asleep in bed before being awoken by the sirens, and she had no doubt the GPS coordinates on her cell phone would match up with her alibi. Meghan had only grown worried when she walked into the station and saw Karen crying on a bench.

"Karen!" Meghan had exclaimed, rushing forward to take her friend into her arms. "What are you doing here?"

Karen had wiped her nose on her sleeve and sniffled. "Officer Nunan insisted I was brought here to talk. Someone overheard our little conversation with Stephanie at her bakery, and they thought I was *serious* when I threatened her! Meghan, you know I wasn't serious; I was just fired up about your recipes. I would never lay a hand on anyone!"

Meghan nodded earnestly. "I know that," she whispered into Karen's ear as they embraced in the police station. "Everyone knows that! You are Sandy Bay, born and raised, Karen. There is surely nothing to worry about. Just tell the police what you were doing last night when the murder happened, and it will be *fine.*"

It wasn't fine. While Meghan's alibi was airtight and corroborated by phone records hastily obtained by the police chief, Karen's whereabouts seemed to be more difficult to trace; she had been signed up to take a midnight yoga sculpt class at the local studio, but she had not shown up to her reserved class time.

"That isn't like Karen," Meghan insisted when Jack informed her of the news. "Karen shows up for *everything*; she is the most dependable woman I know."

Jack shook his head. "I just don't know, Meghan," he said softly as they huddled together in the windowless room. "Her alibi is shaky. She can't seem to give us a straight answer as to where she was, and from the reports of her outburst at Duly Doux….I think we're going to have to book her, Meghan."

"Book her?" she cried, her dark eyes wide in horror. "Jack! She is over seventy years old. She wouldn't hurt a fly! You can't book her."

Jack bit his lip and pushed back his blonde hair. "She *could* hurt someone, though," he argued gently. "She has biceps the size of a horse's! Stephanie was strangled, and it was done by someone strong. Karen is one of the strongest ladies in town….it just doesn't look good."

Meghan frowned. "Can I just talk with her? Please, Jack? She's really upset, and I'm sure I could get some information out of her."

Jack sighed. "I'm not supposed to do that, Meghan, but just this once…."

Meghan leapt up from her chair and hugged Jack. "Thank you," she whispered.

Jack nodded curtly. "Don't mention it. Seriously, I could get in trouble if Officer Nunan finds out I did a favor for you while I was on the clock."

Meghan smiled. "I won't tell. Come on. Let's go find Karen."

Jack led Meghan into the hallway. Karen was still sitting quietly on the bench, but just as Meghan approached her, a clatter broke out.

"She did it!"

Meghan turned to see Trudy, Stephanie's assistant, marching down the hall and pointing a finger at Karen. "She did it! Everyone knows it. She and the girl stormed into Duly Doux and caused a ruckus! Karen even threatened to *kill* Stephanie. Lock her up, officers!"

Karen rose from the bench and glared down at Trudy. "Trudy, how could you say that? You and I go back way longer than you and Stephanie! We're both from Sandy Bay. How could you say something like that about me? Is this because I made the cheerleading squad fifty years ago and you didn't? Trudy! This is ridiculous!"

Trudy wrinkled her nose. "I don't let *murderers* talk

to me like that," she declared. "Stephanie offered me the best-paying job I've ever had, and now *you've* killed her."

Karen frowned. "This is unbelievable," she muttered under her breath. "Jack? Jack, dear, can you please take me home? I answered all of the questions you and Officer Nunan had, and I need to run; I have my evening weights session soon, and I don't want to be late."

Before Jack could speak, another officer walked up to Karen and nodded at her. "You can go now, Ms. Denton," the officer said dryly. "We may need to speak to you again soon, though…."

Karen nodded. "Of course. Meghan? Let's go."

Trudy screeched. "You're just letting her go? Officer, everyone in the bakery *heard* her threaten my boss. Karen Denton is a *killer*, and she said it herself in front of the entire town!"

# 5

THE NEXT MORNING, Meghan's heart sank as she heard a police siren outside of Truly Sweet. She and Karen had been sipping on tea and discussing the events at the police station, and now, Meghan's hands were shaking as two officers stepped out of a squad car and marched into the bakery.

"What are they here for?" Karen whispered. "I thought we told them everything."

Meghan shrugged. "I have no idea," she admitted. "But let's just cooperate; it's been a rough couple of weeks, and I don't want any trouble for either of us."

The little silver bells chimed as the officers walked through the front door. Their heavy, dark shoes were loud against the wooden floors, and Meghan nervously brought her fingers to her mouth and began to chew them as the officers approached.

"Karen Denton?"

Karen nodded at the young, green-eyed officer who stood in front of her. "That's me," she answered.

"I'm Officer Wilberforce," the man said. "Ma'am, I'm going to need to ask you to stand up for me."

As Karen rose from her seat, Officer Wilberforce placed a pair of handcuffs on her.

"What is this?" Karen yelled. "We've already spoken to the police! What's going on?"

Officer Wilberforce shook his head as he tightened the handcuffs. "Ma'am, we have reason to believe that you had something to do with the recent death in town. Our investigators found some charges on your accounts…"

"Charges?" Karen asked. "What charges?"

"A one-way flight from Sandy Bay to Manila," the other officer offered. "For this evening. It seems suspect, and we need to speak with you immediately."

"I was going for a marathon!" Karen protested. "And then traveling! Ask her. She knows!"

Officer Wilberforce frowned. "Ma'am, can you just please come with us? We need to sort this out as quickly as possible."

Meghan jumped as the little bells on the door chimed and Kayley Kane, a local real estate agent, strutted through the door.

"Bad time?" Kayley asked as she looked from Meghan, Karen, and the officers. "I can come back…."

"Let go of me!" Karen shrieked as Officer Wilberforce quickly snapped the handcuffs on her thin wrists and walked her out of the bakery. "You let go of me right now! Meghan? Meghan! This is a mistake!"

Kayley snapped her gum as Karen was taken out of the shop and edged into the police car. "So," she said as she raised her eyebrow. "Bad time?"

Meghan sighed. "It's fine," she answered. "I can grab your order. You had a box of donuts, right?"

"Yeah," Kayley answered as Meghan scurried to the back to retrieve the box. "And I *need* a donut after my day today."

"Oh yeah?" Meghan asked. "What happened?"

"Well," Kayley began as she chewed her gum in annoyance. "I was working on the sale of that new bakery, and well, you know what happened! Real estate just gets sticky when someone dies while a deal is in process, you know?"

Meghan dropped the box of donuts on the floor. "Oh no," she mumbled as she bent down to pick up the box.

"Are you okay?" Kayley asked, then gesturing at the officers who were now strapping Karen into the back of the police car. "What's going on with *her*? Is Karen okay?"

Meghan shook her head. "I don't know, but I need you to repeat what you just told me."

Kayley bit her lip. "About the deal that's fallen through with the dead lady?"

Meghan's face paled. "Yeah. What's up with that, Kayley? Stephanie was *selling* her bakery?"

Kayley shrugged. "The details were murky, but yeah. All I know is that Stephanie Cameron moved to town, bought that bakery, turned it into a wild success, and then, she wanted it out of her hands as fast as I could help her."

Meghan gasped as Kayley reached for the box of donuts. "I *must* be going," Kayley said, turning on her high heels and walking toward the door. "Thanks, Meghan. I'll see you later."

"Wait!" Meghan called out. "Kayley! Wait! You *know* something, and I need to know what that something is *right now*."

# 6

EVEN THOUGH KAYLEY was wearing high heels, Meghan was surprised at how fast she was walking. She had never been a fan of high heels but admired women who wore them, especially for workday functions.

"Kayley, wait!" Meghan yelled as she followed Kayley outside. A gust of salty air blew Meghan's hair into her eyes, and she pushed it back as she moved toward Kayley. Meghan's heart lurched as she saw Karen being loaded into the police car, but she walked toward Kayley with her head held high. "What do you mean, Stephanie wanted the bakery out of her hands?"

Kayley turned and raised an eyebrow at her. "Meghan, I am late for a meeting with a client. I am *leaving*."

Before Meghan could speak, she saw two tiny balls of fur run past her. "Fiesta! Siesta!" Meghan shrieked as she realized her little dogs had gotten loose. "Kayley! Wait! My dogs are following you."

"I don't have time to wait!" Kayley yelled as she stomped away down the sidewalk on her red high heels, the large breeze rolling in from the ocean flipping her skirt to and fro. "I have a client, Meghan."

"Kayley! Look down at your feet!" Meghan shouted.

Fiesta and Siesta had caught up to Kayley, who was fifty feet in front of Meghan. Both dogs were barking good-naturedly at Kayley, but she was perilously close to crushing them with her tall, pointy shoes.

"Meghan, I don't have time for this." she replied.

"Kayley! My dogs are at your feet!" Meghan called out as Fiesta nipped at Kayley's heel.

"Ouch!" she cried, stumbling, and then falling on the sidewalk. The box of donuts tumbled out of her hands, and Fiesta and Siesta began to lick the loose desserts.

"Meghan!" she screamed. "You have to be kidding me. Look at this! Your dogs tripped me, and now, they are eating the treats for my client."

Meghan caught up with Kayley and kneeled beside her. Meghan tried to stifle her laugh as Kayley brushed the dirt off of her expensive leather pants, and Meghan offered her a hand to help her up.

"I'm sorry," she said earnestly as Kayley rolled her eyes. "They mean well. I'll send over some free donuts later, too. I'll make sure you have donuts to last you the *year*, Kayley."

Kayley scowled. "Any other tricks up your sleeve today, Truman? First, you drop the donuts, then you send your dogs after me, and then, they ruin my desserts."

Meghan raised an eyebrow. "Since we're here…." she began. "Can you *please* tell me more about the sale with Stephanie? Please? I'll throw in pies for a year! What do you think, Kayley? I'll send over a fresh pie to your office for you once a week for a year."

Kayley gritted her teeth and looked down at her watch. "Fine," she conceded. "I'll give you two minutes. What do you want to know?"

Meghan bit her lip. "Why was Stephanie selling the bakery? She was doing so well."

Kayley sighed. "She told me that her divorce was going south; she hadn't anticipated it getting so expensive, and her jerk of an ex-husband is--was-- making the finances difficult to sort out. She was going to sell the bakery to pay him off and be done with him forever."

Meghan frowned. "That's terrible," she said quietly. "Poor Stephanie. From what she said, and from what you've told me, it sounds like her ex-husband was a terrible man."

Kayley nodded. "Yeah, Stephanie said he was a player. She said he had a nasty streak and a wicked temper, and that she was afraid of him. I know that she was ready to be done with him, once and for all."

"Done with *who*, ladies?"

Meghan and Kayley turned to find a tall, muscular brunette man glaring at them as he stepped out of a rental car.

"Hello," Meghan said. "Can we help you?"

The man nodded. "Yeah, I think you can. Are you Kayley Kane?"

Kayley nodded. "Yes? Do I know you?"

The man grimaced. "I saw your photograph on the website; you're the real estate agent who is freeing up the money for my divorce."

The color drained from Kayley's face. "And, you are....?"

The man stepped forward toward the women, and Meghan could smell his sour breath as he grew closer. "I'm Jeremy Cameron," he hissed. "Stephanie's husband, or rather, her *ex*-husband."

# 7

MEGHAN PUFFED OUT HER CHEST and stood in front of Jeremy. She had had her fair share of altercations with individuals of questionable character since arriving in Sandy Bay and was not going to be intimidated by the man standing in front of her.

"Why are you here?" Meghan asked him. "Shouldn't you be back in Indiana?"

Jeremy laughed. "And who do you think you are?"

Meghan shook her head. "I was a...friend of Stephanie's," she answered. "It doesn't matter who I am. Who do you think you are, coming around here when Stephanie's been murdered?"

Kayley placed her hands on her hips and glared at Jeremy. "Mr. Cameron," she began, her voice business-like. "I had been working nonstop with my client, Mrs. Cameron, to free up the money you requested. We've been compliant with your demands. Why exactly are you here to see me?"

Jeremy smirked. "Now that Stephanie's gone, everything she had belongs to *me*," he insisted. "I flew here, first-class, to collect my money."

Kayley wagged a finger at Jeremy. "That's for the lawyers to decide," she informed Jeremy. "I don't take orders from you. If your lawyer, or Stephanie's lawyer, wants to give me directions, I will happily take them, but for now, I have no business with you."

Kayley turned and stormed away from Jeremy and Meghan, her hands balled into fists as she walked down the sidewalk.

"Well, wasn't she a treat," Jeremy said sarcastically. "You were a friend of my wife's? Well, what do you know about her assets?"

Meghan grimaced. "I think it's pretty clear what happened to Stephanie," she said evenly as Jeremy watched her. "It's convenient that her ex-husband just happens to show up less than a week after her murder…."

Jeremy crossed his arms. "I loved her," he said softly. "Our divorce was ugly, but I wanted her back. I came all the way here to bring my gal home, and as soon as I arrived, I found out she had been killed."

Meghan shook her head. "If you loved her, you wouldn't be complaining about her assets," she said under her breath. "You would be upset!"

Jeremy narrowed his eyes at Meghan, and she felt her chest tighten. He was a large man, and Meghan was intimidated as he moved closer to her.

"My business is none of *your* business," he declared. "Stay out of my business, and I'll stay out of yours."

Later that evening, Meghan paid a visit to the jail to see Karen. "You're looking tired" she said, surveying Karen's worried eyes. "How are you holding up?"

"Not good," Karen admitted. "They're holding me until they run some lab tests to confirm if any of the DNA found on Stephanie's body was from me. They're saying that given my physique, I could have easily taken Stephanie down and strangled her. It's awful, Meghan. Just awful!"

Meghan held back tears as she stared at her dear friend, clad in a bright orange jumpsuit and sitting behind a thick plastic screen. "I'm so sorry, Karen."

Karen shook her head. "I've been in worse pickles," she assured Meghan. "I know that I am innocent, and soon, after the testing comes back, they will too! My name will be cleared. For now, I just have to get used to nasty jail food and their terrible workout room here."

Meghan laughed. "Only you would be concerned about working out in *jail*, Karen! You are too much. Now tell me, is there anything I can do for you?"

Karen's eyes widened. "Actually, sweetie, I have an idea…."

"Go on," she said.

Karen sighed. "Remember Trudy, Stephanie's assistant? I just have a bad feeling about her. She was so insistent on *my* guilt, and it was clear to everyone in the shop that I was joking about doing away with Stephanie. I just have a notion that she may know something, Meghan. I think you should check her out…"

"Trudy," Meghan said slowly. "Trudy. Jack says she is the one who found the body. She *must* know *something*."

While Meghan could understand why anyone would remotely take Karen's empty threat seriously, she still couldn't shake off the fact that Trudy appeared over dramatic in her outburst at the police station the other day. Could it be she was trying to overcompensate for something or someone involved in this murder investigation?

# 8

MEGHAN BIT HER LIP as she peered into the windows of Duly Doux. She cocked her head to the side when she noticed the lights where on, hoping she would find Trudy, or at least some sort of evidence that would absolve Karen. Her heart pounded in her chest as she noticed the shadows of two figures in the corner of the dining area. Who was in the bakery, and what were they up to?

Meghan slowly pushed open the front door. "Hello?"

Meghan heard a gasp. "What are *you* doing here?" Trudy cried out as Meghan placed her hand over her mouth. Trudy and Jeremy were standing together, his arms wrapped around her waist.

"I'm sorry," Meghan said softly, her dark eyes wide as she looked from Jeremy to Trudy. "I didn't mean to interrupt."

"You *again*," Jeremy groaned as he walked into the back room. "Trudy, I've dealt with her enough. I'm going to run to the store and pick some things up. Be back later."

Meghan cringed as Jeremy slammed the back door on his way out. She looked at Trudy, who was shaking as she stared at Meghan. "That wasn't what it looked like," she said, her voice thin.

"I'm in no place to make judgements," Meghan informed her. "I just wanted to talk with you. May I sit?"

Trudy nodded. "Just be careful," she warned Meghan. "The police said that they are done here, but you never know…."

Meghan nodded. "Of course. I'll be careful."

The two women sat down at a small wooden table, and Trudy looked down at her feet. "It's only been going on for a few days," she confessed to Meghan. "Jeremy showed up in Sandy Bay, and I have been drowning in work trying to keep Stephanie's shop open."

Meghan gave Trudy a sympathetic look. "You don't have to explain," she soothed. "It's been a wild week for everyone."

Trudy began to cry, and Meghan noticed the wrinkles around her hazel eyes. Trudy looked to be a few years younger than Karen, and Meghan couldn't help but to pity the older woman as she rocked back and forth in her chair.

"Trudy," she murmured. "What can you tell me about Stephanie's death? You were the one who found her here, yes?"

Trudy nodded. "I did," she wept. "Stephanie was so good to me. We had our troubles, of course, as any boss and her employees do, but she was a good lady."

Meghan raised an eyebrow. "Troubles?"

Trudy shrugged. "Stephanie had a temper," she began. "She snapped at me a few times, and once, she got in my face when I had painted the wrong letters on a banner. It wasn't pretty."

Meghan bit her bottom lip as she processed Trudy's story. "Did you two ever have any physical altercations?"

Trudy frowned. "I think you've asked enough questions," she said, wiping the tears from her face. "I'm embarrassed you caught me with Jeremy, but I didn't forget that *you* and Karen Denton came in here like a lot of harpies. I think it's time for you to go. If there are questions, the *police* will ask them."

Meghan smiled sweetly and walked to the door. "Thanks, Trudy."

As Meghan closed the door of Duly Doux, she dialed Jack's cell phone.

"Hello?" he answered.

"Jack," Meghan said breathlessly. "Trudy,

Stephanie's assistant, and Jeremy, her ex-husband, were involved in some way!"

"What?"

"Yeah! I walked into Duly Doux, and they were standing close. His arms were on her waist, and they were clearly embarrassed when I caught them."

Jack sighed. "Oh, Meghan…"

"There's more." she cried. "Stephanie was not kind to Trudy; it sounds like Stephanie paid Trudy well, but from what I gathered, they went round and round a few times about the dumbest little things. Maybe it's time you look into Trudy, Jack; she got really mad when I started asking her difficult questions, and I think she may have some answers."

Jack groaned. "Meghan Truman," he said in admiration. "You are going to put me out of a job, someday, Miss Detective. It sounds like Meghan Truman has uncovered some clues for me….again!"

# 9

SOME SHOP OWNERS CAN BE very superstitious about their dealings with the first customer or client at the start of any business day. They believe dealing cordially with that first customer sets the tone for the rest of the day. Meghan wasn't the superstitious type and was ready to confront the first customer that stepped into Truly Sweet with the candidness he or she deserved.

"Can I help you?" Meghan asked sharply as Jeremy barged into Truly Sweet, his face twisted in a grimace.

"I didn't like the way things went down yesterday," Jeremy said slowly as he ran a hand through his dirty brown hair. "What you thought you saw…"

Meghan took a step back as Jeremy strode up to the counter. She glanced around, trying to determine if any of her nearby utensils could be used as weapons in case things turned ugly with Jeremy.

"What you saw...I came into town a few days ago to settle matters with my ex-wife, and when I found out she was dead, I was devastated," Jeremy explained, his face dark. "What you saw....that's only been going on a few days. Trudy and I...."

"It's none of my business," Meghan declared as she threw her hands up in the air. "It's none of my business how you and Trudy conduct yourselves, and I am staying out of it."

Jeremy raised an eyebrow at Meghan. "That's a pretty judgey tone you have there, girl," he hissed at Meghan as he leaned across the counter. "You'd best watch your tone."

Meghan pasted a smile on her lips. "I apologize," she said evenly. "Is there anything else I can do for you today, Mr. Cameron?"

Jeremy smirked. "No, I think that's all," he said as he turned to walk out of the bakery.

"But hey," he said, turning around and walking back to Meghan. "One more thing."

Jeremy reached across the counter and grabbed Meghan's hand. He gripped it tightly, and she cried out in pain as Jeremy squeezed harder and harder.

"Let go of me!" she demanded, writhing in agony as the color drained from her thin, delicate hand. "What are you doing? Stop it!"

"I just want you to understand who you are dealing

with," he whispered to Meghan, staring into her dark eyes as she began to breathe heavily.

"Please!" she pleaded. "Let go of me! You're hurting my hand!"

Jeremy held on even tight, and despite moving her arms back and forth, Meghan could not break free of his grasp. Jeremy gently stroked Meghan's cheek, and she shuddered.

"You're dealing with *me*, dollface," he murmured. "Don't forget it. Stephanie ran away, all the way across the country to get away from me. Don't you forget that when you think about meddling in my business…"

"Hey!"

Meghan breathed a sigh of relief as Jack burst into the bakery. "What are you doing? Get off of her!"

Jack sprinted to Jeremy and smacked his arm away from Meghan. He wrestled Jeremy to the ground, pinning Jeremy's muscular arms behind his back and wrangling handcuffs onto his wrists.

"That's enough," Jack spat at Jeremy. "I've been trying to find you all morning, and here you are, just waiting for me! And with your hands on *my* girl!"

Meghan's heart fluttered as Jack called her *his* girl; their relationship had been moving slowly, and this declaration planted a seed of hope in her excited heart.

"Jack," Meghan said softly as she waved her bruised hand in front of him. "He did this to me! Look at my hand."

Jack kneeled down and stared at Jeremy. "You were just going in for some questioning, but now, I think we'll add some charges to the list," he said venomously. "You're coming with me."

Meghan lowered her shoulders in relief as Jack marched Jeremy out of the bakery. "I'll call you in a few to check on you," Jack assured Meghan as he left. "I'll take care of this hoodlum."

Meghan blew Jack a kiss as he walked outside, and she placed a hand on her heart as she replayed the scene that had just occurred in her bakery. "I can't take another surprise today," she whispered to herself. "There has been too much going on around here. I moved to Sandy Bay for some peace and quiet, and now, I feel like something is happening here every single week."

"Yoo hoo!"

Meghan nearly jumped out of her skin as Kirsty Fisher, one of Sandy Bay's most elegant ladies, sashayed into the bakery.

"Meghan, darling! It's a pleasure to see you. You're looking well," Kirsty cooed as she bent down to kiss Meghan on both cheeks. "You're just the woman I was looking for."

Meghan groaned, but quickly sat up straight and

forced herself to smile. "What can I do for you, Kirsty?"

Kirsty brushed a piece of lint off of her sweater and adjusted the string of pearls that hung just above her collar-bone. "I have a little favor…"

"Oh?"

"You'll be interested. Tomorrow, I am hosting a luncheon for the Sandy Bay Women in Business Forum, and I was wondering if perhaps you would mind giving a little speech? I was going to ask Stephanie Cameron to talk about her bakery, but, you know…."

Meghan grimaced. "Are you sure you want me there?"

Kirsty nodded. "Of course! A little speech from a young businesswoman would be nice….and perhaps a donation to accompany your chat? A donation of treats from Truly Sweet?"

Meghan sighed. "No problem, Kirsty," she said slowly. "It would be a pleasure."

"Wonderful! I'll text you the details this evening," Kirsty chirped as she tossed her blunt-bobbed hair. "Toodles!"

Meghan buried her head in her hands as Kirsty marched out the front door. "A little speech and some free treats," she muttered as she laughed at Kirsty's audacity. She admired Kirsty's confidence and how she had a knack for twisting people's arm to do what she wanted. She had once offered to help Kirsty with an event that ended up putting Meghan in a lot of trouble. They had since made up and she had come to understand that it was just Kirsty being Kirsty and she didn't mean any harm. "What the heck! I might as well just see what this leads to. Who knows what will happen?"

# 10

THE NUMBER OF WOMEN who packed the room for the Sandy Bay Women in Business Forum came as a surprise to Megan. The women in attendance looked the part and she was impressed by all the speakers who took the stage.

"And as women, we should *always* support our fellow women! Female entrepreneurship is one of the most important things we should be focusing on in our society, and we need to commit to each other, ladies!"

"Isn't she spectacular?" Kayley whispered to Meghan as they watched the deputy chair of the Sandy Bay Women in Business Forum, Carol May, finish her impassioned speech.

"She's a local banker who moved here years ago from Indiana. Rumor is that she worked with *Stephanie*

*Cameron* in Indianapolis. Anyway, she is one powerful woman. I'm so happy she agreed to give the keynote address today for the event."

Meghan smiled as Carol waved her hand in the air. Carol appeared to be in her mid-forties, but she had the energy and enthusiasm of a teenager, along with the refinement of a queen. Meghan was eager to formally meet her after the event, and she had begged Kayley to introduce them after Carol's address.

"My bank will support any ventures of female entrepreneurs. That is my promise to you, ladies!" Carol announced to the audience of cheering women.

"She helped my cousin, Tara, get a loan to start her candle shop," Kayley explained to Meghan as the crowd applauded. "I can't wait to introduce you."

After the address, Kayley whisked Meghan away to a corridor in the back of the auditorium.

"She'll come this way when she walks off stage," Kayley explained. "She'll remember me from the real estate deal I did for her son last autumn, don't you worry!"

Meghan smiled. "Thanks for offering to introduce me," she said as she pulled Kayley into a hug. "Especially after my pups…."

"Don't mention it," Kayley responded as she snapped her gum. "Women need to support women, just like Carol said, yeah?"

Meghan grinned. "That's right!"

Kayley nodded as thunderous applause signified the end of Carol's speech. "Okay, look!" Kayley exclaimed. "There she is. She's coming this way."

As Carol walked down the corridor in her sleek green suit and matching skirt, Meghan could not help but to stare in awe. Carol walked with confidence, and she smiled graciously at everyone she passed. Meghan hoped that someday, she too would exude the same sort of elegance that Carol had.

"Hey! Carol!" Kayley called out as Carol passed. "Carol? It's Kayley. Kayley Kane?"

Carol stopped in front of Kayley. "Kayley Kane!" Carol beamed. "So lovely to see you. How are you doing in that real estate business? I see your pretty, powerful face on all of the billboards in town. You must be doing well!"

Meghan smiled as Kayley blushed. "Business is going well," she admitted. "And my cousin's candle shop is thriving as well. You helped her get the loan to start her business."

Carol nodded. "It's always been my passion to help empower female business owners, and I was so pleased to help her."

Kayley shoved Meghan in front of her. "Carol," Kayley said. "This is my friend, Meghan Truman. She owns Truly Sweet, that bakery on the square."

Carol took Meghan's hands in hers and squeezed them. "Meghan Truman! What a thrill it is to meet you," she purred as Meghan studied her face. "I was out of town when you started that bakery of yours, but I have just loved following its progress in the papers. You are quite the accomplished businesswoman in Sandy Bay."

Meghan felt the color rise in her cheeks. "That is so kind of you to say," she said to her. "It hasn't been easy, but it has been worth it."

Carol nodded. "It's never easy being a woman in today's world, but if we stick together, we can achieve great things."

Kayley agreed. "Yes! And Meghan is accomplishing her own great things at the bakery. Rumor is she has a few corporate orders running right now?"

Meghan's shoulders sagged. "I had some setbacks," she admitted as Carol gave her a look of sympathy. "When Stephanie Cameron's bakery opened, I lost some of my corporate orders. It's been a slow run the last few weeks…"

Carol rolled her eyes. "I hate to sound naughty," she whispered into Meghan's ear as Meghan's eyes widened. "But I have a little secret."

Meghan leaned in. "What is that, Carol?"

Carol winked at Meghan. "I've tried desserts from poor Stephanie Cameron's bakery, and I've had a few things from your place here and there, Meghan,"

Carol began. "I must say, that despite her successes, I truly thought that *your* treats and *your* bakery was-- and is--better than Stephanie Cameron's, bless her soul."

Meghan could not keep the smile off of her face as Carol squeezed her hands. "I don't mean to be irreverent of poor Stephanie, but your compliment means the world, Ms. May!" Meghan gushed.

"Please," Carol insisted. "Call me Carol."

"Carol," she repeated. "Carol. Well, Carol, thank you for the kind words and for taking the time to talk with me. I loved your speech, and I can't tell you how much your words inspired me to be the best businesswoman I can be!"

"Not a problem at all, dear," she replied, winking once more at Meghan. "It's truly sweet to impart wisdom upon young ladies such as yourself and Ms. Kane. Ladies, it's been a pleasure. Have a wonderful day, and enjoy the rest of the event."

Meghan's jaw dropped as Carol floated away. "She's amazing!"

Kayley placed her hands on her hips and shook her head. "That was weird," she said as she furrowed her brow.

"What was weird?" Meghan asked as she turned to Kayley. "She was so gracious and nice."

Kayley shook her head. "It doesn't make sense…."

"What doesn't make sense?"

Kayley wrinkled her nose. "What she whispered to you about Stephanie's bakery….it didn't make sense."

Meghan cocked her head to the side. "What are you talking about, Kayley?"

Kayley pursed her lips. "It's just weird that she would insult Stephanie's bakery especially considering the fact that Carol May was Stephanie's business partner."

# 11

"AND SHE SAID THAT Stephanie and Carol were *business partners*, Jack!" Meghan said into her cell phone as she walked home from the event. "I don't understand."

"It makes sense, Meghan," Jack responded as Meghan twirled a loose strand of dark hair around her finger. "Carol May is one of Sandy Bay's most influential female entrepreneurs. She loves taking an interest in businesswomen, and from what I know, she and Stephanie once worked together in Indianapolis. Their connection probably goes back way longer than we know. I wouldn't sweat it."

Meghan sighed. "You're probably right," she admitted. "I'm just trying to look at every angle here, Jack. Karen is still sitting in jail, and I'm on edge about her being with all of the criminals and crooks day after day."

Jack laughed. "Oh, Karen Denton is being well-taken care of," he assured Meghan. "Officer Nunan arranged for her to have a private room. It's one of our nicer spots, and Karen has been doing plenty of yoga, pilates, and jump-roping."

Meghan giggled. "That lady….she is something."

Jack's voice grew serious. "I do have something to tell you, though," he said. "I think we're on to the real culprit, Meghan."

"What? Who do you think it is, Jack?" she asked.

"Jeremy. The ex. It just makes sense," Jack explained. "He comes into town, he was still attached to Stephanie's life insurance policy and from what my team has found out, he has a massive amount of debt waiting for him all across the Midwest! Jeremy has been in serious need of quick cash, and it seems likely, given his history, that he would use Stephanie to pay his way out of his messes."

Meghan gasped. "That's terrible! Who could do such a thing?"

Jack sighed. "The things people do these days, Meghan," he replied sadly. "It's awful how desperation can drive someone to do a terrible thing. I just hope we can charge him and move things along quickly. The DNA test still hasn't come back yet, and we have to keep Karen until we have some hard evidence against Jeremy. It could still be a few days until we can let her out…."

Meghan groaned. "Ugh! Jack, are you *sure* Jeremy is the culprit?"

Jack cleared his throat. "What are you suggesting, Meghan?"

Meghan paused, taking a long inhale as she unlocked the front door to her bakery. "I just have a bad feeling about Jeremy, but I don't think he killed Stephanie," she confessed.

"Well, Detective Meghan, who do you think did it?" Jack asked. "Trudy? Karen?"

"I don't know yet," Meghan admitted. "But I will find out. Just give me some time, Jack. Give me some time, and I will find out who killed Stephanie Cameron."

"Okay, Meghan," he said slowly. "But be careful, please. I don't want you to put yourself in any danger. I like having you around Sandy Bay, Meghan, and I wouldn't want anything to happen to you!"

"Don't you worry about me, Jack," she said confidently. "I'm *brave*, Jack Irvin. I'm braver than even I know, and I will find out who killed Stephanie Cameron, once and for all!"

# 12

AS MEGHAN HUNG UP the phone with Jack, she glanced across the street at Duly Doux. It was nearly ten in the evening, but the lights were on.

"What is going on over there?" she asked herself as she walked back outside of Truly Sweet. "Jeremy is in jail right now, but is Trudy still over there at this time of night?"

Meghan gripped her phone tightly as she walked across the street. She slowly pushed open the door to Duly Doux and gasped. "Carol?"

Carol May stood in the middle of the bakery, her green outfit still looking fresh even after the long event. "Meghan Truman! Twice in one day. What a pleasure. What are you doing here?"

Meghan smiled at Carol and walked over to shake her

hand. "I live across the street, just above my bakery," she explained. "I saw that the lights were on over here, and I wanted to come check it out. I thought perhaps Trudy was over here?"

Carol shrugged. "Trudy? Hmmmm. She's away, actually."

"Oh!" Meghan replied. "That explains why I didn't see her at the event tonight."

Carol nodded. "I'm not sure if Kayley mentioned it, but I actually own part of this bakery," she said softly as she looked around Duly Doux. "It's such a shame that Stephanie met such a terrible end before she could get this place off of the ground. I came over to take a look around and to try and decide where to go from here. Do I sell this place? Do I keep it? Decisions, decisions!"

Meghan nodded sympathetically. "Her death was quite unexpected," she said quietly. "She and I had some...words before her death. I try to be a friend to everyone, but I was frustrated with her. I think Stephanie copied down some of my recipes when I wasn't looking, and from what I've been told, she used them in Duly Doux…"

Carol frowned. "Women can be so hard on each other," she said, reaching to gently pat Meghan's shoulder. "It's hard to be a woman in business. I'm sure Stephanie was just jealous of your many successes. I'm terribly sorry she stooped to such a low level."

Meghan smiled at Carol. "You've been so kind to me. I wish I had met you when I first moved here; I could have used all of your advice."

Carol laughed. "I wish I had been here, but I think you have handled things well. Your business model seems to be working--despite the little Stephanie roadblock--and you seem like a nice girl. I think you're going to be just fine."

Meghan's heart warmed as a loud pinging noise rang from the kitchen of Duly Doux. "Is that the oven?" Meghan asked Carol as she turned on her heel and walked into the kitchen. "I'll go turn that off for you."

"No!" Carol yelled, but it was too late; Meghan screamed as she turned into the kitchen and tripped over Trudy's motionless body.

"Trudy? Trudy!" Meghan wailed. "Carol? What happened here?"

Carol sprinted to Meghan and tackled her, with Meghan consequently hitting her forehead on the edge of the counter.

"What are you doing?" she screamed as Carol pulled Meghan's dark hair.

"You've seen too much," Carol said matter-of-factly as she swung her legs around to straddle Meghan's middle. "You can't leave now, Meghan. I'm sorry. I truly liked you, but…."

Meghan coughed as the weight of Carol's body

crushed her lungs. She looked over at Trudy's body and saw a large bruise on her neck. Trudy was still, and her eyes were rolled back in her head.

"What did you do to her?" Meghan cried out as Carol tugged at her hair. "Why did you hurt her?"

Carol let go of Meghan's hair and gazed down into her eyes. "She knew too much, too," she answered. "Trudy was at the wrong place at the wrong time, just like you, Meghan."

Meghan kicked and fought as Carol reached into her pocket for a long, pointed dagger. "You killed Stephanie, didn't you, Carol?" Meghan asked as Carol grabbed for her throat. "You strangled her and left her here for Trudy to find!"

Carol lowered herself closer to Meghan's face. "So what if I did?" Carol said venomously as she waved the dagger around with one hand. "So what if I did? Stephanie and I have known each other for *years*, and even after I had given her my time, my financial backing, and my counsel, she was going to sell this place out from under me!"

"What?" Meghan screeched.

"She wanted to sell this place to pay out her divorce, and she didn't bother telling me," Carol said calmly. "I found out by accident, and I was horrified. This place was making money, Meghan, and she wanted to just throw it away. I confronted her, of course. I told her that Duly Doux's opening day sales proved that she had the potential to be the premier bakery in the

Pacific Northwest. This place was a hit!"

Meghan's dark eyes widened. "What did she say?"

Carol grimaced. "She didn't care. She just wanted to settle her affairs and get out of this business. She lacked a backbone, Meghan, and now, I wish I hadn't invested in her. She lacked the true marks of an entrepreneur, and I'm embarrassed I got involved. Stephanie couldn't even make her own treats; she had to steal *your* recipes. She was pathetic, that woman!"

Meghan's eyes widened as Carol slowly lowered the dagger to Meghan's throat, rubbing the edge along the bottom of Meghan's chin. "Just be still," Carol advised Meghan. "Be still, and it won't hurt....much."

Meghan tried to wriggle out from under Carol, but she could hardly move. "Why?" Meghan asked Carol. "Why?"

"Stephanie and I were colleagues in Indianapolis years ago, and when she reached out to me to move to Sandy Bay, I was happy to help her," Carol explained, her eyes flashing with rage. "I wanted to help her; I knew her husband was no better than trash, and I hoped Stephanie could have a fresh start. She failed here, though; she was not confident, and she lacked business acumen. I knew she wouldn't succeed. When Kayley Kane mentioned that Stephanie was planning to sell Duly Doux after only *weeks* on the job, I knew that something had to be done. She lacked grit, Meghan. Female entrepreneurs need *grit* to survive in this difficult world!"

"It's a good thing I have grit!" Meghan shouted as she mustered her strength to push Carol off of her. Carol shrieked as she landed in the puddle of blood next to Trudy's body. "My suit! My green suit! You've stained this skirt, Meghan Truman! This was my power suit. You'll be sorry…"

Carol lunged for Meghan, but Meghan kicked her left leg high, sending the knife flying across the room. Carol jumped on Meghan, and they rolled around on the laminate floor, blood covering their clothes as they wrestled to gain control.

"I've got you now!" Carol yelled triumphantly as she climbed onto Meghan's chest. "I hate to do this to a successful businesswoman, but like I've said, you have seen too much. I wish Stephanie had been tougher, I wish Trudy's timing had been better, and I wish you hadn't meddled. But, it isn't useful to dwell on the past, so…."

Carol brought her hands to Meghan's neck and began to squeeze. "Meghan, it's been a pleasure," she said as Meghan began to choke. "This will be quick, I promise…"

Suddenly, just as Meghan's vision began to fade, there was a loud crack from the doorway. Carol collapsed onto Meghan, and Meghan filled her aching lungs with air.

"Meghan!"

Meghan heard her name shouted as she fell into the dark, warm tug of unconsciousness.

# 13

THE FALLOUT FROM Carol May's murder of Stephanie was devastating to the reputation of the local bank she represented. An internal investigation was launched by the board of the bank and it was discovered that she facilitated loans to some individuals of questionable character. Much worse was the fact that she accepted kickbacks for issuing these loans. It also came out in the investigation that Carol had used her influence to persuade Majestic Incorporated to cancel their order with Truly Sweet and divert it to Stephanie's bakery. The bank had to put a publicity plan in place to win back the confidence of the citizens of Sandy Bay as the news of Carol's escapades spread far and wide. As Meghan looked back on the events of the past few weeks, she was grateful that she didn't have any business dealings with Carol or her bank.

"And Trudy wasn't dead! She was just unconscious, and she knocked out Carol before Carol could strangle me." Meghan exclaimed as she drove Karen away from the Sandy Bay Jail. "It was awful, Karen; I really liked Carol, and seeing her lay there, unconscious on the floor….it was a lot to take in."

Karen clucked sympathetically. "We've *both* had difficult weeks. You had to tussle with Carol and solve the mystery for your detective, Jack, and I had to sit in a jail cell."

Meghan laughed. "It all sounds crazy, but it's just life in Sandy Bay, isn't it?"

Karen shook her head. "I thought moving back here would mean some quiet and peace," she said. "Maybe the quiet and peace is still coming?"

Meghan nodded. "It *must* be! I'm ready for some rest and relaxation after the last few weeks."

Karen turned to look at Meghan's bruised neck. "She really got you, didn't she?"

Meghan sighed. "She did," she whispered. "It was so scary, but I fought so hard, Karen."

Karen frowned. "Between Carol and Jeremy, you have had to be one brave lady recently."

Meghan blushed. "I just did what I had to do, Karen," she said. "Everyone can be brave when the time is right."

Karen reached over and patted Meghan's head. "I have no doubt, sweetie," she said. "You are a fabulous, brave woman! I am proud of you for doing everything you did to help me and to solve the mystery."

Meghan smiled at Karen. "You are such a dear friend to me," she said. "I would do anything for you, Karen."

"By the way, do you know what happened to Jeremy, Stephanie's ex?

"Jack said they received an arrest warrant for him from the police force in Indiana. Apparently, he had a stack of misdemeanors he had to answer. Jack and his team were happy to see the back of him and processed all the paperwork in record time. I believe he should be back in Indiana as we speak."

Karen gestured outside as they pulled up in front of Truly Sweet. "Look at that, Meghan," Karen said gleefully. "Jack Irvin is waiting for you."

Meghan's jaw dropped as she saw Jack outside. He was dressed in a navy suit and holding a bouquet of pink roses.

"What is going on?" Meghan asked as Karen shook her head.

"Why don't you go find out?"

Meghan unbuckled her seatbelt and ran out of the car. Her heart was pounding in her chest, and she could feel the butterflies in her stomach as she approached Jack. She shivered in the cool evening and took a long breath, taking in the salty air coming into the town from the ocean.

"Jack!" Meghan exclaimed. "Why are you so dressed up? What is going on?"

Jack smiled down at Meghan, and she felt a wave of heat rise in her belly as she stared into his blue eyes.

"Meghan," he said softly. "Meghan, you were in danger *twice* this week, and I have been so worried about you!" he began. "Seeing you hurt and stepping in when that Jeremy fellow was in the bakery made my blood boil. It helped me see what was in front of me."

Meghan bit her lip as she gazed into Jack's eyes. "What is that, Jack?"

Jack held out the roses to Meghan. "These are for you."

"Thank you!" Meghan squealed as she buried her nose into the sweet-scented flowers. "You are too nice to me, Jack."

Jack pursed his lips and took a long breath. "Meghan," he said softly. "Meghan, you have been right in front of me this entire time. I've loved getting to know you, and I've loved spending time with you, and I want to ask you a very important question."

Meghan felt butterflies in her stomach as Jack grinned. "Yes, Jack?"

"Meghan," Jack breathed. "Will you be my girlfriend?"

Meghan gasped. "Jack," she said softly as she rushed into Jack's strong arms. "That would be truly sweet."

**The End**

*Eclairs and Lethal Layers*

# Afterword

Thank you for reading Eclairs and Lethal Layers! I really hope you enjoyed reading it as much as I had writing it!

If you have a minute, please consider leaving a review on Amazon.

**Many thanks in advance for your support!**

# About Finger Foods and Missing Legs

**Released**: October, 2018
**Series**: Book 6 – Sandy Bay Cozy Mystery Series
**Standalone**: Yes
**Cliff-hanger**: No

Meghan Truman is ecstatic when she discovers she's won an all-expense paid trip to Paris for a Food and Baking convention. She's never been to Europe and is looking forward to the sights, smells and people.

Her trip takes a very sour turn when one of the chief conference speakers is reported missing and subsequently found dead in her hotel room. Meghan is shocked when she's informed she has been identified as a person of interest who the police want to speak to.

With her European trip in danger of turning into her worst nightmare, she must quickly identify who had the most to gain from the victim's demise and absolve herself of any link to the murder before her hopes of closing a lucrative deal fade away in the city of Love.

# FINGER FOODS AND MISSING LEGS
# CHAPTER 1 SNEEK PEEK

MEGHAN TRUMAN'S HANDS SHOOK as she pulled a bulky yellow envelope out of the mailbox. She had been eagerly awaiting this correspondence for *weeks*, and as she carried the envelope inside of Truly Sweet, her bakery, Meghan's dark eyes grew wide in excitement.

"Finally," Meghan whispered as she reverently placed the envelope on the front counter. "The news I have been waiting for!"

"Meghan! Meghan, can you come help me?"

Meghan stifled a sigh as Trudy, her new assistant, called out to her from the kitchen. She peered at the envelope, her heart thudding in her chest as she admired the elegant handwriting on the front proclaiming it to be *hers*.

"Trudy, can it wait?" Meghan asked as she ran her fingers along the edges of the yellow envelope. "I have some mail I need to read; I've been waiting for this letter for months, and it's *finally* here!"

Meghan heard a loud crash from the kitchen, and she begrudgingly left the envelope on the counter to tend to Trudy. Her new assistant had been working at Truly Sweet for only a few weeks, and usually, the two women got along well; while Meghan was a twenty-seven year old transplant to the Pacific Northwest, and Trudy had lived in Sandy Bay all of her life, the pair worked well together, and Meghan was thrilled that she had help at the bakery. Truly Sweet was the only bakery in Sandy Bay, and while Meghan loved running her business, it was hard work, and Trudy had proven to be an asset to the business.

"What's going on, Trudy?" Meghan asked as she burst into the kitchen. "Are you alright?"

Trudy was a mess; she was covered in flour, and there were bowls and cutlery scattered on the tiled floor. "I had a little fall, Meghan! I'm alright! Just a little trip."

Meghan laughed in spite of herself. "You poor thing," she said kindly. "Let me help you up; I'll give you a hand, and we can tidy the kitchen before the morning crowd comes in."

Trudy smiled. "Sorry, boss. I'll be more careful next time."

The two women worked together to clean the kitchen, both exchanging jokes and stories as they swept the flour from the cracks of the floor, scrubbed the dishes, and put things in order.

"There!" Meghan said thirty minutes later as they surveyed their work. "Much better."

Trudy grinned. "I have news for you, Meghan; it's never a boring day at Truly Sweet, that's for sure!"

Meghan gasped. "News! News! I had forgotten! The news I've been waiting for arrived today, Trudy. I have to go open that envelope."

Meghan raced back to the dining area to retrieve her envelope. Trudy followed behind her, and she clucked as Meghan tore open the yellow paper. "I haven't seen you this excited since that sweet Jack Irvin asked you to be his girlfriend a few weeks ago," Trudy said as Meghan shook with excitement. "You were adorable, Meghan; I had never seen someone so happy to be off the market."

Meghan beamed. Jack Irvin, a local detective, was everything she had dreamed of in a boyfriend; he was handsome, intelligent, confident, ambitious, and kind, and Meghan had grown quite fond of him in the five months she had lived in Sandy Bay. Jack had helped Meghan through some unexpected troubles with the bakery, and Meghan was thankful for his support.

"You were jumping around the bakery like a little girl after he asked you. He *is* a catch; I've watched Jack Irvin grow up, and that boy is a sweetheart! You're a lucky girl, Meghan, but Jack is a lucky guy, too. You two are a cute couple."

Meghan grinned. "I do feel pretty lucky," she admitted. "When I moved to Sandy Bay from Los Angeles all of those months ago, I didn't know what would happen; opening the bakery was a challenge, and making new friends in town was certainly daunting, but now, I am so happy. I have a thriving business, wonderful friends, an amazing assistant, and a new boyfriend!"

Trudy winked. "And hopefully some good news! Open that envelope, Meghan. I'm dying to know what's in there."

Meghan ripped open the top of the envelope and began to read the letter aloud.

*Dear Meghan Truman,*

*We are pleased to inform you that you have been selected to attend the LeBlanc St. James Food and Baking Convention in Paris, France. You have been selected from a pool of over ten thousand finalists, and we are elated to extend this invitation to you to join us in Paris for the convention.*

*All of your expenses will be taken care of at the LeBlanc St. James Food and Baking Convention; we have enclosed a voucher for your airfare, as well as your reservation information for your complimentary stay at Grand Hôtel du Palais Royal, a five-star hotel located in one of the city's finest neighborhoods.*

*We looked forward to seeing you at the convention. Thank you for your interest in the event.*

*Je vous remercie,*
*The Selection Committee of the LeBlanc St. James Food and Baking Convention*

Meghan's jaw dropped. "I'm going to Paris, Trudy!" Meghan screamed as she began jumping up and down. "I'm going to *Paris*!"

Two weeks later, Jack packed the last of Meghan's suitcases into the trunk of his undercover car. "Are you sure you need three bags?" Jack asked as he held the passenger door open for Meghan. "That's going to be a lot to keep track of in Paris."

Meghan shrugged. "I've never been to Europe before," she said giddily. "I want to look my best in Pa-reeeee!"

Jack laughed as he settled into his seat and began driving toward the airport. "I don't know if I've ever seen you so excited. It's adorable, Meghan. I'm so happy for you."

Meghan blushed. "Thanks, Jack. And thank you for taking me to the airport today."

Jack reached over and took Meghan's hand. "That's what boyfriends are for, right? Anyway, it just means I get to spend more time with you. This might sound a little silly, but I'm going to miss you while you are away."

Meghan bit her bottom lip, feeling her face grow hot as Jack looked at her. She could feel butterflies in her stomach, and she felt her lips turned upward into a smile as Jack's blue eyes stared at her. "I'm going to miss you too, Jack. We haven't been apart for more than a few days, but I know that we'll manage this week with no problem! We can chat every evening, and I can even put some postcards in the mail for you!"

Jack squeezed Meghan's hand. "I just feel protective of you, Meghan," he admitted. "You are very special to me, and it makes me nervous to think of you gallivanting in Paris. If something happens to you, I can't save the day and make sure you are okay."

Meghan felt tears brim in her eyes, and she was warmed by Jack's sincerity. "I'll be careful, Jack. I want to come home to Sandy Bay--and to you--in one piece."

Jack nodded. "Just promise you'll stay out of trouble while you're away?"

Meghan leaned over and kissed Jack's cheek. "I promise," she assured him. "I'll be busy at the convention each day, and it's only a few blocks from the hotel. I'm going to do a few sightseeing tours, but those are guided, so I think I'll be in good hands."

Jack squeezed Meghan's hand again. "This sounds like an amazing experience for you," he breathed as Meghan studied his serious face. "I'm so proud of you, and I can't wait to see your beautiful face coming toward me at the airport in just a few days."

Two hours later, Meghan waved goodbye to Jack as she walked into the security line. She made it through security in no time, and before she knew it, she was buckled into her window seat on the airplane. Meghan leaned back, enjoying the hustle and bustle of the passengers boarding the plane. She ordered a soda from the flight attendant, and once it was delivered, she sighed.

"It's almost time," Meghan whispered to herself as she gazed out the window. "It's almost time to start my adventure in Paris! I wonder what this week will bring….."

You can order your copy of **Finger Foods and Missing Legs** at any good online retailer.

A SANDY BAY **6** COZY MYSTERY

*Finger Foods and Missing Legs*

AMBER CREWES

# ALSO BY AMBER CREWES

## The Sandy Bay Cozy Mystery Series

Apple Pie and Trouble

Brownies and Dark Shadows

Cookies and Buried Secrets

Donuts and Disaster

Éclairs and Lethal Layers

Finger Foods and Missing Legs

Gingerbread and Scary Endings

Hot Chocolate and Cold Bodies

Ice Cream and Guilty Pleasures

Jingle Bells and Deadly Smells

King Cake and Grave Mistakes

Lemon Tarts and Fiery Darts

Muffins and Coffins

# Newsletter Signup

Want **FREE** COPIES OF FUTURE **AMBER CREWES** BOOKS, FIRST NOTIFICATION OF NEW RELEASES, CONTESTS AND GIVEAWAYS?

GO TO THE LINK BELOW TO SIGN UP TO THE NEWSLETTER!

**www.AmberCrewes.com/cozylist**

Amber Crewes

# Eclairs and Lethal Layers

Manufactured by Amazon.ca
Bolton, ON

14271573R00053